ملائكة ألفي

ALFIE'S ANGELS

In memory of Alfons,
who taught me about angels. H.B.

For Mum, Dad and Daniel,
for your support and encouragement. S.G.

First published 2003 by Mantra Lingua
Global House, 303 Ballards Lane, London N12 8NP
www.mantralingua.com

Text copyright © 2003 Henriette Barkow
Illustrations copyright © 2003 Sarah Garson

This sound enabled edition published in 2013

British Library Cataloguing in Publication Data:
a catalogue record for this book is available from the British Library.

ملائكة ألفي

ALFIE'S ANGELS

Henriette Barkow

Sarah Garson

Arabic translation by Dr Sajida Fawzi

MANTRA LINGUA

أراد ألفي أن يكون ملاكاً.
كان قد رآهم في كتبه.

Alfie wanted to be an angel.
He'd seen them in his books.

كان قد رآهم في أحلامه.

He'd seen them in his dreams.

Angels have wings and angels can fly.
Alfie wanted wings so he could fly to
school on time.

الملائكة لها أجنحة وتستطيع أن تطير.
أراد ألفي أن يكون له إجنحة لكي يطير إلى
المدرسة ويصل في الوقت المضبوط.

Angels can dance, and sing in beautiful voices.
Alfie wanted to sing so that he could be in the choir.

الملائكة تستطيع أن ترقص وتستطيع أن تغني بأصوات جميلة.
أراد ألفي أن يغني لكي يكون في الكورَس.

تتحرك الملائكة بسرعة أسرع ممّا تراها العين.

Angels can move faster than the eye can see.

أراد ألفي أن تكون حركته أسرع كي
يستطيع أن يحقق أهدافاً أكثر.

Alfie wanted to move faster so
that he could score more goals.

الملائكة تأتي بكل الأشكال ...

Angels come in all shapes...

... وبكل الأحجام.

...and sizes,

ويستطيعون أن يفعلوا أغرب الأمور.

and they can do the most amazing things.

أراد ألفي أن يكون ملاكاً.

Alfie wanted to be an angel.

كان قد رآهم في كتبه.
كان قد رآهم في أحلامه.

He'd seen them in his books.
He'd seen them in his dreams.

والآن يستطيع الأطفال أن يكونوا ملائكة مرة واحدة في السنة. يختارهم المعلمون. الآباء يُلبسونهم الملابس اللائقة. وتشاهدهم المدرسة كلّها.

Now once a year children can be angels.
The teachers choose them.
The parents dress them.
The whole school watches them.

Alfie's teacher always chose the girls.

كانت معلّمة ألفي تختار البنات دائماً.

تختار البنات الجميلات. تختار اللواتي لهن أطول شعر.
واللواتي لهن أكبر عيون وأحلى ابتسامات.

The prettiest girls. The girls with the longest hair.
The girls with the biggest eyes and the sweetest smiles.

But Alfie wanted to be an angel.
He'd seen them in his books.
He'd seen them in his dreams.

ولكن ألفي أراد أن يكون ملاكاً!
كان قد رآهم في كتبه.
كان قد رآهم في أحلامه.

وعندما سألت المعلمة "من يريد أن يكون ملاكاً؟"
رفع ألفي يده.

When the teacher asked,
"Who wants to be an angel?"
Alfie put up his hand.

ضحكت البنات بصوت عالٍ. وضحك الأولاد خِلسة.

The girls laughed. The boys sniggered.

حملقت المعلمة في نظرها. ثمّ فكرت وقالت:
"يريد ألفي أن يكون ملاكاً؟
ولكن الملائكة هم بنات فقط".

The teacher stared. The teacher thought and said, "Alfie wants to be an angel? But only girls are angels."

وهزّ ألفي رأسه ببطء.
وكان قد و أخبر معلمته كلّ شيء عن الملائكة.

Alfie slowly shook his head,
and he told his teacher all about the angels.

كيف أنه كان قد رآهم في كتبه.
كيف أنه كان قد رآهم في أحلامه.

How he'd seen them in his books.
How he'd seen them in his dreams.

وكلما تكلم ألفي أكثر كلما استمع إليه تلاميذ الصف أكثر.

And the more Alfie spoke,
the more the whole class listened.

لم يضحك أحداً لا بصوت عال ولا خلسة، بسبب رغبة ألفي ليكون ملاكاً.

Nobody laughed and nobody sniggered,
because Alfie wanted to be an angel.

Now it was that time of year when children could be angels.
The teachers taught them. The parents dressed them.
The whole school watched them while they sang and danced.

والآن حان ذلك الوقت من السنة الذي يستطيع فيه الأطفال أن يكونوا ملائكة. علّمتهم المعلمة. ألبسهم الآباء الملابس اللائقة. وشاهدتهم المدرسة كلها وهم يغنون ويرقصون.

وهكذا كان ألفي ملاكاً!

Alfie was an angel!